LEABHAIR E[...]

Deirdre agus an Fear Bréige
ÚNA LEAVY

Siné[...]
Da[...]

Sailí ag Spotaí

Bróga Thomáis
ÚNA LEAVY

Dána
AINE NÍ GHLINN

Fiacla Mhamó

An tUan Beag Dubh

Lámhainní Glasa

Mo Mhadra Beoga
PATRICK DEELEY

An Buachaill Bó
GILLIAN PERDUE

An Rún Mór

Cá Bhfuil Murchú?
ANNA DONOVAN

Scuab Fiacal Danny

Do Conor, mo dhearthráir beag cúileáilte

An Buachaill Bó

Gillian Perdue

• Léaráidí le Michael Connor •

Leagan Gaeilge: Daire Mac Pháidín

THE O'BRIEN PRESS
DUBLIN

An chéad chló 2006 ag
The O'Brien Press Ltd,
12 Terenure Road East, Rathgar, Dublin 6, Ireland.
Fón: +353 1 4923333; Facs: +353 1 4922777
Ríomhphost: books@obrien.ie
Suíomh gréasáin: www.obrien.ie
Cló speisialta do Lá na Leabhar Dhomhanda 2010

ISBN: 978-1-84717-186-3

1 2 3 4 5 6 7 8 9 10
10 11 12 13 14

Faigheann The O'Brien Press cabhair
ón gComhairle Ealaíon

Eagarthóir: Daire Mac Pháidín
Dearadh leabhair: The O'Brien Press Ltd
Clódóireacht: J F Print Ltd, Sparkford, Somerset

Thaitin buachaillí bó
go mór le Conor.
Bhí go leor eolais aige faoi
bhuachaillí bó ó leabhair
agus ón teilifís.

Bhí capall mór, láidir
ag gach buachaill bó.

Chaith siad téada
agus bhéic siad:
'*Yee haw*,' agus '*Giddy-up.*'

Chodail buachaillí bó
amuigh faoin spéir
agus chan siad amhráin
cois tine.

Ach an rud ba mhó
a thaitin le Conor
ná a gcuid éadaí.

9

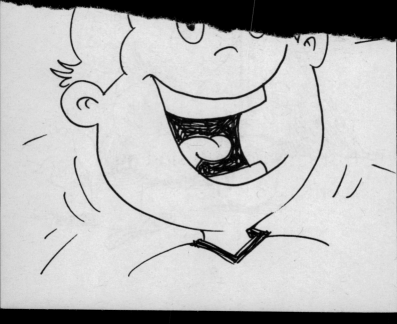

Thaitin an hata mór
leathan a chaith siad go
mór leis.

Thaitin an scairf bheag
a chaith siad
timpeall a muineál
go mór leis.

12

Nuair a bhí stoirm
ghainimh ann tharraing an
buachaill bó an scairf thar a
bhéal agus a shrón chun an
gaineamh a choinneáil
amach.

Chaith siad brístí géine
agus bástcótaí cúileáilte.

Agus chaith siad 'chaps'
(brístí speisialta leathair)
thar na brístí géine.

Chaith buachaillí bó
buataisí móra le spoir.

Agus níos fearr fós
bhí crios speisialta acu
don dá ghunna airgid.

Chaith Conor an lá ar fad
ag súgradh mar bhuachaill
bó.

Agus bhí brionglóidí ag
Conor gach oíche faoi
bhuachaillí bó.

Tharraing sé pictiúir
de bhuachaillí bó
agus dhathaigh sé isteach
a gcuid éadaí
go cúramach.

Ansin, lá amháin,
tharla rud éigin iontach.

Cheannaigh Mamaí agus
Daidí bronntanas speisialta
do Conor.
Tháinig sé i mbosca
an-mhór.

Bhí an bronntanas ina shuí
ar bhord na cistine.

Bhí Mamaí agus Daidí
agus a dheirfiúr mhór Laura
ag fanacht leis
chun an bronntanas a
oscailt.

Stróic Conor an páipéar den
bhosca agus thosaigh sé ag
screadaíl.

Ansin thosaigh sé ag léim
suas agus anuas.

'Culaith buachalla bó!' a
bhéic sé.
'**Go hiontach**!'

Chuir sé an bríste air ar
dtús.

Ansin chuir sé an bástcóta
air. Bhí trí chnaipe airgid
air agus bhí póca beag
ar an dá thaobh.

Cheangail sé an scairf
timpeall ar a mhuineál.
Ansin chuir sé an hata mór
leathan ar a cheann.

'*Howdy*, Maw,' ar seisean.
'*Howdy*, Laur'.'
Thosaigh siad ar fad ag
gáire.

Ansin chuir sé an crios
leis na gunnaí air
agus tharraing sé
an dá ghunna amach.

'Lámha suas!' a bhéic sé ar Dhaidí. 'Ná maraigh mé,' a bhéic Daidí ag cur suas a lámha.

Ní raibh lá níos fearr ag Conor riamh.

Ní raibh Conor sásta
an chulaith buachalla bó
a bhaint de
an oíche sin.

Ach bhain, ar deireadh.
Ansin chuir sé a éadaí
codlata air –
agus an chulaith buachalla
bó os a gcionn.

Bhí go leor brionglóidí aige
faoi bhuachaillí bó an oíche
sin.

B'shin an oíche ab fhearr
a bhí aige riamh.

Dhúisigh Conor go luath
an chéad mhaidin eile
chun dul ar scoil.

Bhain sé an chulaith
buachalla bó agus a éadaí
codlata de. Ansin chuir sé a
éide scoile air – agus an
chulaith buachalla bó
os a chionn.

Chuaigh sé síos go dtí an
chistin.
'*Howdy*, gach duine,' a dúirt
sé.

Stop an chlann ar fad ag
ithe. 'Ní féidir leat an
chulaith sin a chaitheamh
ar scoil,' arsa Laura leis.
'B'fhearr duit an chulaith
sin a fhágáil sa bhaile,' arsa
Daidí leis. 'Conor!' a
thosaigh Mamaí. 'Ní ...'

'Táim ag caitheamh
mo chulaith buachalla bó
ar scoil,' arsa Conor.

'Ach …' arsa Mamaí, Daidí
agus Laura.

'Ná habair rud ar bith eile,'
arsa Conor.
'Nó gheobhaidh mé mo
ghunnaí.'

'Beidh siad ag magadh fút!'
arsa Laura leis.

Ach lean **Conor an
Buachaill Bó** ar aghaidh ag
ithe a bhricfeasta.

Thug Mamaí Conor
agus Laura ar scoil.
Bhí Laura ag caitheamh
éide scoile. Bhí gach páiste
eile ag caitheamh éide scoile
freisin. 'Bain díot an

chulaith sin sula léimeann
tú amach as an gcarr,'
arsa Laura leis.
'Ní bhainfidh,' arsa Conor.

Thug Mamaí a mhála scoile
agus a lón do Conor.
'An bhfuil tú cinnte
faoi na héadaí sin?'
a d'iarr Mamaí air.

'Feicfidh mé tú
agus an ghrian ag dul faoi,
Maw,' a dúirt Conor léi.

Bhí go leor páistí
ag stánadh ar Conor.
'An bhfuil tú ag dul ag
cóisir?' a d'iarr siad air.

Ach shiúil **Conor an
Buachaill Bó**
díreach ar aghaidh.

Shroich Conor doras
an tseomra ranga.
Dhírigh sé a hata.
Chuir sé a lámha
ar a chuid gunnaí
agus shiúil sé isteach.

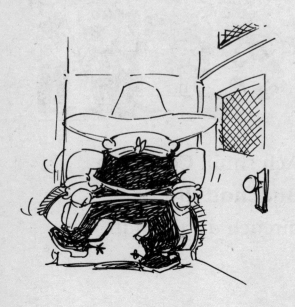

D'fhéach na páistí ar fad
suas. Stop an chaint
sa seomra ranga.
Bhí siad ar fad ag stánadh
air.

'*Howdy,*' arsa Conor leo.

Shiúil Conor chuig a bhord
go mall réidh.
Bhain sé a mhála scoile de
agus chuir sé ar an urlár é.

Bhain sé a hata de
agus chroch sé
ar chúl a shuíocháin é.

'*Howdy*, Ma'am,'
a dúirt sé lena mhúinteoir,
Niamh. Ní dúirt Múinteoir
Niamh ach:

'Eh … eh …'
'Is mise **Con an Buachaill
Bó**,' arsa Conor léi
agus meangadh mór gáire
air.

Ag am lóin chuaigh
Con an Buachaill Bó
amach sa chlós.
Bhí go leor páistí
ag iarraidh súgradh leis.

'*Yee haw,*' a bhéic siad,
ag bailiú na mbó.
'*Giddy-up.*'
Bhí spraoi iontach acu.

Theastaigh ó gach duine
an chulaith buachalla bó
a chur orthu.

'Is liomsa í seo!' arsa Conor.
'Tóg do chulaith féin ar
scoil,' a dúirt sé le gach
duine.

Ach chuala Múinteoir
Niamh é.

'**A thiarcais**!' a dúirt sí
léi féin.
'Beidh tríocha buachaill bó
agam amárach!
Cad a dhéanfaidh mé?'

Dúirt cairde Conor
– Sinéad, Ciarán agus Marc
– go raibh siad chun
teacht isteach gléasta
an chéad lá eile.

'Tá mise ag teacht isteach
mar shióg,' arsa Sinéad.
'Tá gúna álainn agam sa
bhaile.'

'Tá culaith rince agam,'
arsa Marc. 'Tá sí cúileáilte.'
'Culaith rince!' a dúirt siad
ar fad le hiontas.
D'inis Marc dóibh go raibh
sé ag iarraidh bheith i
mbanna ceoil nuair a
bheadh sé níos sine.

Ní dúirt Marc mórán
faoin rince riamh mar go
mbeadh na buachaillí eile
ag magadh faoi. 'Is breá
liom rince,' ar seisean.
'Feicfidh sibh mo chulaith
rince amárach.'

Bhí culaith saighdiúra ag
Ciarán. 'Tá buataisí
iontacha agus clogad
speisialta agam!'
a d'inis sé dóibh.

Chuala Múinteoir Niamh
an chaint ar fad.
Bhí comhrá beag aici le
Conor ag am lóin.

Tar éis am lóin sheas Conor
suas chun fógra a
dhéanamh.

'Amárach Dé hAoine,'
a dúirt Conor.
'Is féidir le gach duine
gléasadh gach Aoine as seo
amach.'

Bhéic na páistí ar fad le
háthas. 'Maith thú, **Con an
Buachaill Bó**,'a bhéic siad.
'Beidh spraoi iontach
againn.'

D'inis Conor an scéal ar fad
do Mhamaí, Laura agus do
Dhaidí an oíche sin.

'Níl sé sin féaráilte,' a dúirt
Laura, 'Ba mhaith liom
gléasadh freisin.'

'Caith do chulaith asarlaí
ar scoil amárach,'
a dúirt Conor léi.
'B'fhéidir!' arsa Laura leis.

Bhí go leor daoine aite
i rang Conor an lá sin.

Bhí **Con an Buachaill Bó**
ann.

Bhí **Marc**
an rinceoir
iontach ann.

Bhí **Sinéad**
an tsióg álainn ann.

Agus bhí **Ciarán**
an saighdiúir ann.

Bhí:

diabhal

aingeal

moncaí

píolóta

agus píoráidí

An Príosún

Agus cé a bhí ag barr an ranga?

AN SIRRIAM!

Bhí lá iontach ag na páistí
an lá sin.
Bhí lá iontach
ag Múinteoir Niamh fiú!

Bhí asarlaí amháin i rang
Laura – bhí éide scoile ar
gach duine eile.

Ach thosaigh siad ag caint
ag am lóin.
'Gléasfaimid gach Aoine
freisin,'
arsa na páistí le chéile.

'Smaoineamh Conor a bhí ann,' arsa Laura.

'Is deartháir iontach tú,' a dúirt sí leis níos déanaí. 'Is **deartháir cúileáilte** tú!'

Shéid Conor an deatach
óna ghunna.

Bhrúigh sé siar a hata.

'*Gee!* Go raibh míle', Laur'.'

'Home time!' she said. 'Mary, go and get the coats, please. Anna, I'd like a little word with you.'

Mrs Winkle's voice dropped. She leaned so close to me that I could see the fine white hairs poking out of her nose.

'I know what *really* happened to your home-work today. You were fooling about with magic and it went wrong!'

You see, Mrs Winkle knows all about me being a witch. And the reason she knows all about me is simple.

It's because Mrs Winkle – head teacher of St Munchin's, keen golfer, church bell-ringer, and well-respected figure in the community – is *also* a witch!

The Witch in the Woods by Marian Broderick, ISBN 978-1-84717-108-5

AVAILABLE IN ALL GOOD BOOKSHOPS

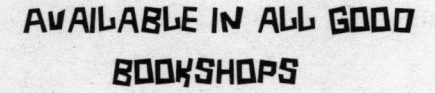

www.obrien.ie

doesn't know I'm a witch. (After all, no-one wants to be the class *weirdo!*)

I took what was left of her workbook and went to find her. She was sitting under the hazel tree in the playground.

'Mary,' I said. 'I'm really sorry!'

'Why?' she said. 'What have you done?'

'I'm afraid I accidentally dropped your book out of the window,' I lied. 'And all the homework pages blew away.'

'You WHAT!' said Mary. 'Oh, Anna! Now we'll *both* get detention!'

And that's exactly what happened. We were kept back after school, and Mrs Winkle marched us into detention. I was worried Mary might crack and tell Mrs Winkle what I'd done – but I should have known better. She's loyal and she kept her lips zipped.

*   *   *

After half an hour of detention torture, Mrs Winkle took off her glasses, polished them, and stood up.

work or not. It's a bit unreliable when you're a beginner. But this time, it was instant. I felt power surge through my legs and out through my fingers. There was a flash of blue light, and numbers started to float off the workbook pages.

Yippee! I thought. *It's working!*

The numbers hovered in the air. The 2s and 3s started bumping into each other while the 1s formed a line and marched up and down. The 0s tried to eat the 3s and then the 4s, so the 5s got scared and started whizzing about really fast. Meanwhile the 8s and 9s just wobbled on the spot.

Then, to my horror, the whole lot – including all the pluses and minuses – flew across the classroom and straight out of the window.

I ran to the window and stared after the tiny figures. They bounced and swirled away across the playground, over the trees, and disappeared from sight.

I looked back at the workbooks. They were both completely blank!

What was I going to tell Mary? I couldn't tell her about the magic spell, of course, because she breaktime, there was *loads* of copying to do! It was going to take all day!

And that's when I decided to give myself a little extra help – *magic* help!

You see, I'm a natural-born witch. Or, to be more precise, I'm a natural-born witch who doesn't like doing her homework – *any* homework, whether it's magic homework or normal homework.

Being a witch and being lazy is not a good combination – especially when you're only an apprentice like me. It makes you do really stupid things – like what I did next.

I took our workbooks and locked myself into an empty classroom. I chalked a star shape on the floor and jumped inside. Then I opened both our workbooks, placed them on a desk, pointed one finger at each of them and made up a rhyme:

Boring sums and squiggly signs
Copy from her book into mine!

I never really know whether a spell is going to

1. ANNA'S MAGIC MISTAKE

Last Thursday started off like any other Thursday. First I overslept, then Aunty Grizz marched around the kitchen telling me off, while Aunty Wormella tried to shovel porridge into my mouth. Finally, I raced out of the house to school, buttoning my shirt as I ran.

As the iron gates of St Munchin's clanged shut behind me, I had a horrible thought: My maths homework was due in this morning, and I'd forgotten to do it *again*!

Mrs Winkle, our head teacher, was definitely going to *kill* me this time. So as soon as I could, I grabbed hold of my best friend, Mary.

'Can I copy your maths homework into my workbook at break?' I whispered during register.

'Forgotten it again, have we?' she smiled. 'Yes, of course you can.'

But when I looked at her workbook at

READ ANNA'S SECOND
ADVENTURE, THE WITCH IN THE
WOODS.
TURN THE PAGE TO READ THE FIRST
CHAPTER...

AN

ANNA
THE WITCH

BOOK!

A BOOK OF MISCHIEF
AND MAGIC ...

MARIAN BRODERICK is a nasty lady who has written many **unpleasant** books for The O'Brien Press. She claims she isn't a witch, but her kitchen is always full of **green smoke**, and she has been spotted dancing with cats in the moonlight. Her hobbies are polishing her warts, singing like a crow – and **forcing** little children to dig up her garden. If you see her, **run away** very fast!

'ANNA THE WITCH' BOOKS
THE WITCH APPRENTICE
THE WITCH IN THE WOODS
A WITCH IN A FIX

THE
WITCH
APPRENTICE

MARIAN BRODERICK

ILLUSTRATED BY FRANCESCA
CARABELLI

THE O'BRIEN PRESS
DUBLIN

For Isabel, Eoin, Fabio and Adriana

First published 2007 by The O'Brien Press Ltd,
12 Terenure Road East, Rathgar, Dublin 6, Ireland
Tel: +353 1 4923333; Fax: +353 1 4922777
E-mail: books@obrien.ie; Website: www.obrien.ie
Reprinted (new edition) 2008.
This special World Book Day edition published 2010.

ISBN: 978-1-84717-186-3

A catalogue record for this title is available from the British Library

1 2 3 4 5 6 7 8 9

10 11 12 13

The O'Brien Press receives assistance from

Layout and design: The O'Brien Press
Printed and bound in the UK by J F Print Ltd, Sparkford, Somerset.
The paper in this book is produced using pulp from managed forests.

CONTENTS

LEAVING SUNNY HILLS

I couldn't believe my eyes when I first saw number 13 Crag Road. No wonder everyone at the Sunny Hills Children's Home had sniggered when I'd said it was going to be my new home.

Everything about number 13 was crooked. Its walls were crooked, its chimneys were crooked. Even its doors and windows were crooked.

It looked like it was

going to fall over any second.

But crooked or not, number 13 was my new home. You see, the two ladies who owned the place, Grizz and Wormella Mint, had adopted me.

My name's Anna Kelly. I don't have any parents, and I have never had a proper home. I've been at Sunny Hills Children's Home since I was a tiny baby. By the time I was nine, so many people had decided NOT to adopt me that I had grown used to the idea of spending the rest of my life at Sunny Hills.

But I wasn't happy about it, not one bit. Well, *you* try sleeping six to a room in a big old barn of a place, and see how much *you* like it. You couldn't call anything your own at Sunny Hills!

So when Grizz and Wormella turned up, promising me a pink-and-white bedroom with its own private bathroom, a posh new school, new clothes, weekly pocket money and my own TV, I felt like I'd won the Lotto!

They had been *so* sweet in Mrs Pegg's office. *So* sweet and *so* keen to have me. Very, very keen.

'Anna, darling,' the skinny one had cooed. 'You'll have the run of the house! You'll be able to do exactly as you like!'

'Thanks, Miss!' I said.

'Call me "aunty", dear,' she crooned.

The run of the house! Able to do what I wanted! That suited me just fine. I was used to a lot of rules and regulations at Sunny Hills. It was porridge at 7.00am, lights out at 9.00pm, that kind of thing.

But *now*! Now life was looking up! The two old dears' only wish was to pamper me. I'd get new clothes, new toys ... and I'd be going to the nicest school in town, St Munchin's!

I'd always *really* wanted to go there. The place had everything – outings, after-school clubs, and sports. Lots and lots of sports. This was brilliant because I was mad keen on football – and I wasn't bad at it either, if I do say so myself.

All in all, St Munchin's sounded like something out of a storybook.

'It's a brand new start for you, Anna Kelly,' Mrs

Pegg said, as she bundled me into the cab with the two ladies. She bent and put her lips close to my ear.

'*Don't* muck it up!' she hissed. 'Do as you're told. Keep your room tidy. And above all, Anna …' Mrs Pegg's voice dropped to a whisper. '*Try* to keep that stubborn streak of yours under control!'

Stubborn? Me? Just because I had staged a sit-down protest to force the management to give us chips every Friday. It wasn't my fault the whole of Sunny Hills joined in …

So I promised Mrs Pegg I'd be a model child – and I had every intention of keeping that promise. This was my big chance, and it was going to get me out of Sunny Hills for good.

I must admit, though, I had a lump in my throat when I looked out of the back window of the car, and saw Mrs Pegg wiping her eyes with her hanky. She wasn't a bad old stick, after all – and she was the closest thing I had to a mother.

But I swallowed hard, faced the front, and thought about the fantastic new life ahead of me.

It took exactly a minute after arriving at number 13 Crag Road for me to realise I'd made a mistake. A big, BIG mistake.

*   *   *

As soon as the front door slammed behind me, my two new aunts changed. Especially Grizz, the skinny one.

In Mrs Pegg's office, Grizz had been kindness itself, all smiles in every direction. Now she planted herself in the hallway and pointed a long fingernail up the gloomy stairs.

'Right,' she barked. 'Show the girl to her room, Wormella.'

The *girl*? Was that meant to be *me*? What happened to 'Anna, darling'?

'Yes, sister,' piped Wormella.

In contrast to Grizz, who seemed to have grown taller and pointier since she got home, Wormella seemed to shrink into a small, pudgy ball. She pattered up the stairs in front of me,

leaving me to carry my heavy bags by myself.

My bedroom turned out to be a tiny, dusty little attic with bare floorboards. No TV, no wardrobe, and no bathroom. Just a hard little bed and a

battered cardboard box to keep my things in.

I was horrified.

'Aunt Wormella,' I began – but she had disappeared down the stairs without another word.

It didn't take long to settle in – there wasn't room to swing a hamster, let alone a cat. I wandered back downstairs to the brown, dirty kitchen and peeped through the open door.

The two sisters were sitting hunched over a wooden table, giggling like naughty schoolgirls. The air was foggy with the steam that poured from a huge, black cauldron bubbling on the cooker.

'Now that we've got a dogsbody to do all the dirty work,' Grizz was saying to Wormella. 'Our spells are bound to start working!'

Dogsbody? Dirty work? *Spells*? What were they talking about?

'Ahem!' I coughed.

The aunts looked up, startled.

'Have some nettle tea, dear,' said Wormella quickly. She handed me a chipped mug and a

plate. 'Help yourself to bread and butter.'

I sat down and took a bite of the bread. It was gritty like it was made out of gravel or something, and the butter on top wasn't yellow – it was *grey*.

I gulped a mouthful of tea. That was disgusting too, and tasted like nettles mixed with wee, but at least it washed down the bread.

'Thank you,' I said, and tried to smile as I pushed the mug and plate away.

'Right, girl, rules of the house,' barked Grizz. 'Number one: you will work hard. Number two: you will work hard. Number three: you will work hard.'

Grizz howled with laughter at her own joke and then folded her arms.

'That's all,' she said. 'Goodnight.'

And that was that. The end of my first day in my new home.

2

ANNA'S NEW HOME

That was six weeks ago, and since then, things have gone from bad to worse.

Instead of the new trainers and jeans I was promised, I was given a pointy black hat, black dress, black apron and black boots.

Instead of going to St Munchin's and making lots of new friends, I was up at dawn every day, *working*. I'm only nine, and even *I*

know that's against the law.

The aunts didn't care. They had me cleaning the house, digging up the garden, and slaving over the cauldron. They made me cook really horrible food, such as beetle legs in jelly and toenail toffee, and then bottle it. The food we ate was disgusting too. On a typical day, we would eat fish eyes on toast, live worm salad, and eel pie with slime on the side. There was never a sausage or a chip in sight.

But worst of all, I never got to speak to a soul, except Grizz and Wormella. The only friend I had was Charlie, a black cat. He took a liking to me after I gave him my fish eyes.

Sometimes, when I was working in the kitchen, I'd look out of the window and see a blonde girl, about my own age, walking down the street. She

wore a St Munchin's blue uniform and she looked really cool. I'd see her playing with friends or riding her bike, and I'd wave and try and get her attention, but she never saw me. So I'd sigh and carry on working.

One morning, in the kitchen, the aunts were hunched over some stained yellow papers, and I was stirring the boiling black cauldron as usual.

'This one sounds good, Wormy,' said Grizz, licking her thin lips. 'Tree-beetle custard. Yum yum. It's been ages since we had some of that.'

'Yes, sister,' twittered Wormella, who rarely said anything else.

Grizz shot me an evil look.

'We can send the girl out to get tree beetles tonight,' she said. 'She can go after dark, when it's nice and quiet in the woods.'

My grip tightened on the wooden spoon. This was the last straw: Nice and quiet? More like spooky and DANGEROUS! I stopped stirring, whipped out the spoon and flung it across the dingy kitchen.

It soared over the heads of Grizz and Wormella, and missed Charlie by a whisker.

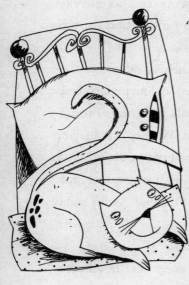

'That's it!' I shouted. 'That is finally, definitely, *totally* IT!' I took off my pointy black hat and threw it on the floor.

'*What* did you say?!' roared Grizz. She pointed one of her talons at me. 'How *dare* you!'

'If you think I'm going to spend my life stirring beetles in this stupid cauldron – you can think again!' I shouted.

'Pick up that spoon and get on with your work, girl!' said Grizz. 'Or else!'

'Or else *what*?' I was so cross I didn't care what I said. I made two fists with my hands.

'I won't do it! I've had enough!' I shouted. 'I

don't know what's going on here, but I'm just an ordinary girl and I *should be in school*, not boiling to death in this dump!'

Grizz leapt from her seat and stalked towards me, while Wormella hid her fat face in her frilly apron.

'*School*?' shouted Grizz. 'Do you think we adopted you from that dirty little kid's home so you could swan about at *school*?'

That was typical. She was always going on about how I should be grateful for being rescued from Sunny Hills. As if it was *my* fault I didn't have any parents. As if Sunny Hills wasn't much, much nicer than Crag Road.

'At least at Sunny Hills, I had friends,' I shouted. 'But here, I have *nobody* except Charlie – and he's not even human!'

Charlie jumped from his seat and wound himself around my ankles.

'No offence, Charlie,' I said.

'*Friends*?' said Grizz. 'We're witches! We don't have friends, we have victims!'

She threw her head back and cackled long and loud. My blood froze in my veins and even Wormella seemed to cower away from her sister.

So *that* was it. Grizz had finally admitted what we were all doing. Witchcraft! And I was helping! I tried to face Grizz down.

'Look at this kip!' I said, waving my arms around the kitchen. 'It's disgusting! And I don't believe you have the first clue what you're doing. Witches – ha! – you're *rubbish*!'

I took off my black apron, threw it on top of the

black hat and stamped on them both.

There was a sharp intake of breath from Wormella. Grizz's face darkened in fury and her eyes narrowed to slits.

'Ungrateful little …!' shouted Grizz. 'Wormella made that specially!'

'And that's another thing,' I said. 'We all look like we're at a funeral. What have you done with my real clothes? Where are my jeans?'

'Witches don't wear jeans, dear,' said Wormella.

Grizz whipped a black wand out of her apron pocket, and pointed it at me, chanting:

'Short and freckly on the rug,
Turn this girl into a slug!'

Nothing happened – if you don't count the fact that my heart nearly stopped in fright. You see, although I didn't believe in witchcraft, these two looked pretty convincing.

Still, I needed to put on a brave face, so I cocked my head on one side and folded my arms.

'Told you so,' I said. 'You're not very good, are you?'

'Oh, hellfire!' shouted Grizz. She threw down her wand and rushed at me, seizing me by my ponytail and dragging me towards the stairs. Wormella trotted after us, getting in the way.

'Oh dear, Grizz,' Wormella said. 'You're not going to leave her in the cellar?'

'Stand back, Wormella,' Grizz said. 'This little twerp needs taming. A few hours in the dark should do it.'

I stifled a whimper. Oh no, I thought. Not the dark – anything but the dark ...

Grizz pushed past Wormella, opened the cellar door and threw me down some stone steps into a black, musty dungeon.

'School, indeed! Waste of a young witch's time!' said Grizz.

'I'm ... *not* ... a ... witch,' I shouted, thudding to the bottom of the steps. 'And neither are you, Grizz, whatever you may think!'

'Don't touch anything!' said Grizz. She

flounced out, slamming the door and bolting it on the outside. I sprang to my feet, ran to the door and pounded on it.

'Let me out!' I shouted. There was no answer, except the sound of laughter ...

3

THE CELLAR AT CRAG ROAD

I slid to the floor and hugged my knees, feeling the cold seep into my bones. It was completely silent – except for something scuttling somewhere in the dark. A chill shot up my spine.

'Hello?' I said in a quavering voice. 'Anyone there?'

A soft miaow broke through the darkness. An instant later, two golden eyes and a black, furry shape crept out of the gloom.

'Charlie!' I said, breathing a sigh of relief. 'You nearly gave me a heart attack!'

I settled Charlie on my lap. He gazed up at me and purred.

'You do understand, don't you, Charlie?' I

whispered. 'It's nothing personal, but I need to make friends of my own kind.'

Charlie nuzzled my chin in reply.

I peered into the dark and wrinkled my nose. The whole place smelt rotten, like a dead hedgehog that's been out in the sun too long and has gone all maggotty. I slid my hand down to the floor. It felt slimy ...

I leapt to my feet and Charlie fell off my lap, yowling in protest.

'It's all right for *you*, grumpy,' I said. 'Us mere humans can't see in the dark. I could be sitting in anything.'

Charlie padded down the steps, towards the middle of the room.

'Hey, wait for me!' I shouted after him in sudden panic. I followed the sound of purring until I heard him jump onto something. His eyes gleamed in the darkness, guiding me towards him. I groped the flat surface around Charlie until I found a box that rattled. 'Please let this be a box of matches, and not a box of rat

bones,' I muttered.

They were matches. I lit match after match, until I found a dusty candle. I lit it and my mouth fell open as I gazed around the cellar in the flickering light.

Brownish liquid was running down the walls and cobwebs hung in long strings from the ceiling. The scuttling sounds I'd heard were cockroaches feasting on piles of rubbish. There were large stars and circles chalked all over the stone floor.

In one corner, hanging from the ceiling like a mobile, was a human skeleton. A fat, hairy spider sat in the centre of its web between the rib bones. Both spider and skeleton swung slowly, back and forth, back and forth …

What a dump! This must be where Grizz tried out her spells. I started shivering – and not just from the cold.

Charlie miaowed. He was picking his way along some kind of worktop. As he stepped over a massive jumble of jam jars and sauce bottles, one

of them spilled over and some stinky, green, gooey stuff oozed out. It smoked and sizzled on the worktop.

I watched, with fingers pinching my nose. The green goo ate its way right through the solid wood and dripped onto the stone floor.

'Come away *now*, Charlie!' I shouted. 'That's *acid!*'

I hopped over the acid puddle to the worktop. On it lay a huge, black book with sharp, metal corners. It had silver letters on the cover, and it bulged with stained, yellow pages.

I inched closer and reached out my hand to open it …

Just then, Charlie yowled and leapt off the worktop. He flattened himself to the floor and crept towards a dark corner, tail waving. I put the candle on the worktop and crept after him.

'What is it, boy?' I said. 'Can you smell something?'

In the corner were several large, square shapes, under filthy covers. I lifted a corner of one cover

and peered underneath.

Six pairs of beady yellow eyes stared back at me through the glass wall of a fishtank.

I leapt back so fast I fell over Charlie, who arched his back and spat at the tank. I picked myself up and pulled off the cover.

The tank was home to at least a dozen hissing green snakes. I pulled off more covers to discover heaps of cages and buckets and tanks. They were packed with animals of all shapes and sizes.

Some of the cages held black rats, some held white mice, and some held scraggy-looking guinea pigs. The other tanks were full of slithering worms and snakes.

One of the snakes was eating its breakfast – it turned to stare at me and I saw the tail of a rat sticking out of its mouth.

But the last bucket I uncovered was the worst. It was full to the brim of wriggling, squirming maggots.

I put my hand over my mouth and backed away fast – I was sure I was going to be sick. I turned from the animals to the worktop. Once

again, the black book caught my eye.

Was it my imagination, or had it moved towards me ...?

Charlie jumped up and sniffed around the book's metal edges – but, straight away, he started hissing and spitting and going mental. I looked at the silver letters on the book's cover.

'*Ancient Evil: Spells for All Occasions,*' I read.

Great. A magic book. And not just any old magic book – an *evil* magic book. It was plain that this was

where all Grizz's stupid recipes and potions came from.

I opened *Ancient Evil* in the middle, and started reading.

Broomstick Potion
At dead of night, dig up three weeds,
Combine with blood and
river reeds,
Add beetle brain and
lizard jaw,
Add snotflakes, wee
and one rat's paw;
Paint your bot with
all this mix
To give some speed to
your broomsticks!

'Paint your *bot*?' I said. 'That's just plain disgusting.'

I turned the pages. What a load of rubbish! Witchcraft – ha! As if

anyone in the twenty-first century was going to fall for that!

'Watch me, Charlie,' I said.

I started to cackle and rub my hands together, just like a real witch. Charlie's round eyes went rounder. I picked up the heavy book and walked around with it, reading aloud another spell in my best cracked, witchy voice:

'To see what kind of witch you are,
Stand inside a pointed star.
Read this spell out loud and clear,
Making sure no humans hear;
If you feel the shaking earth,
It means you've been a witch since birth!'

I looked down at Charlie and laughed. We had wandered inside one of the chalk stars on the floor, so I raised my foot to step out – and then I felt it.

A burning sensation started in the soles of my feet, and worked its way up into my whole body.

'Whoah!' I shouted. 'What's happening?'

An electric shock shot through me. I screamed and looked down.

The ground beneath me had started to move!

Charlie yowled and leapt onto my leg, as the floor began to shake more and more violently. The floor churned up and down, and glass bottles crashed from the shelves to the ground.

'Charlie!' I shouted. 'Get out! Get out of the star!'

I dropped the book and stumbled out of the star, with Charlie still digging his claws into my leg. Instantly, the ground stopped shaking.

But I didn't. Not for a long, long time.

4

MEETING MARY

By the time Wormella came and rescued me from the cellar, I had just about recovered from the shock of what had happened.

I spent the whole sleepless night turning it all over in my mind. Was this loony bin sending me crazy – or was I, Anna Kelly, a real, live, witch, like the spell said? And if I *was* a witch, could *I* do magic spells?

Soon a plan started to take shape in my brain.

The next morning, I sneaked back into the cellar and ripped out some pages from *Ancient Evil*. I went into the garden where I was supposed to be collecting nettles and snail slime in a bucket. But, instead, I was secretly looking at the pages I'd stolen.

Maybe I could make one of these evil potions,

and give Grizz and Wormella a taste of their own
medicine!

'Hello!' said a cheerful voice.

I jumped and spun around. A face was peering over the back fence. It was the blonde girl from up the road!

She smiled and I smiled back at her.

'Do you live here?' she said. 'Or are you just visiting?'

'I live here, unfortunately,' I said. 'The two mad old witches took me from a children's home so I could do all their dirty work ...'

The girl giggled. She obviously thought I was joking.

'You're funny!' she said. 'My name's Mary. What's yours?'

'Anna,' I said. 'Where do *you* live?'

'Down the road,' said Mary. 'You should come over and play sometime.'

'I'd love to,' I said. 'But, somehow, I don't think I'll be allowed.'

Mary looked me up and down.

'Is *that* your school uniform?' she asked.

'No!' I said. 'What kind of school would have an all-black uniform?'

We both looked at my witchy black dress and pointy boots and burst out laughing.

'Where *do* you go to school anyway?' asked Mary.

'I don't,' I mumbled.

'You don't go to *school*?' said Mary, shocked. 'How come?'

'I'm not allowed,' I said.

'I go to St Munchin's,' said Mary. 'It's *so* much fun. You should get your aunts to send you there! We might be in the same class ... Ooops!'

Without warning, Mary dropped to her knees behind the fence.

'You, girl!' shouted a sharp voice from behind me. 'What do you think you're doing?'

I turned. Grizz was striding across the garden.

'Who were you talking to?' she said.

'No one,' I said. Mary didn't need to get in trouble as well. I was in enough for both of us.

Grizz looked over the fence. Mary was nowhere to be seen.

'Get back to work instantly,' said Grizz.

I put on my gloves and grabbed my bucket of nettles.

'You wait and see, Grizz!' I said. 'I'm going to go to school, and make friends, and have normal life!'

'Over my dead body!' shouted Grizz.

'Don't tempt me!' I muttered, as my hand curled around the pages of spells in my pocket.

5

THE FIRST SPELL

That night, my dreams were full of St Munchin's. Mary and I were walking to school together, wearing beautiful, blue St Munchin's uniforms ...

And then I was in a large hall, accepting a prize on prize day. People were applauding and shaking me by the hand until it felt it might drop off, but still they were shaking and shaking and shaking ...

I opened one eye. Grizz's thin face was pushed close to mine and she was shaking my shoulder.

'Wakey, wakey,' she growled.

Outside the attic window, the first streaks of light were showing above the chimneys. She had to be kidding.

'It's only just dawn!' I said.

'So?' said Grizz. 'Get up. There's work for ungrateful girls to do. It may not be *schoolwork*,' she said, curling her top lip, 'But it's good enough for the likes of you.'

Grizz stamped out of the attic and down the stairs. I knew she'd be back in five minutes in a raging temper, so I groaned and struggled out of bed.

Down in the kitchen, the cauldron was already on the boil. Charlie was sitting on the windowsill, washing his face.

'Hello, boy,' I said, reaching out to tickle Charlie's ears.

'Leave him alone and get on with your work!' said Grizz, slapping my hand away. 'I want baked toad for lunch. And I want a potion for killing next door's flowers.'

'Next door's flowers?' I said, rubbing my hand. 'But why? They're about the only pretty thing in this street.'

'*That's* why,' said Grizz. 'Now. Chop these

earwigs and mix them with some granny's toe-nails, cow dung ...'

I stopped listening. I was thinking of my plan.

'Wormella,' said Grizz. 'Where's The Book?'

'In the cellar, dear,' replied Wormella.

Grizz gave Wormella a hard look.

'Sorry, dear,' said Wormella, 'I meant the lab.'

Grizz bustled off downstairs, muttering. Wormella followed, leaving Charlie and me alone in the kitchen.

I whipped out the crumpled pages I had hidden in my apron since yesterday. I flicked through them until I came to one that said 'Sleeping Potion'.

'That's the one,' I said.

Sleeping Potion
To make a sleeping potion strong,
Pull thirteen hairs, both brown and long,
Add juice of slug, and broken rocks,

And nightshade root, and poo of fox.
Into a drink, the mixture seep,
To make the victim go to sleep.

From the windowsill, Charlie realised what I was up to, and sat up straight, like a bookend. His eyes widened, and he watched my every move.

'Don't panic, Charlie,' I said. 'I'm not going to *kill* anyone – not today, at least. I bet it doesn't even *work*, anyway!'

I ran my finger along the kitchen shelves.

'Now, what do we need? Slug juice and broken rocks …'

'What was that, dear?' said Wormella, wandering back into the room.

I nearly dropped dead on the spot. She scared the life out of me, creeping around like that.

'I was just saying, Aunt,' I said, 'That we're low on slug juice.'

'Well spotted, dear!' said Wormella. 'You see! You're getting the hang of witchcraft, after all!'

'Actually,' I snapped. 'I don't *want* to get the hang of it!'

Wormella ignored me. She gave the cauldron a half-hearted stir and drifted into the garden.

'That was close, Charlie,' I said. 'I'll have to be quick before she comes back. Go and keep watch.'

Charlie leapt from the windowsill and sat in the back doorway. I poured the slug juice into a jug and mixed it with the broken rocks. I got down a jar of night-shade root and grated some into the jug. Then I held my nose as I mashed in a dried lump of fox poo.

'We'd better be careful with this,' I muttered. 'It *is* poisonous, after all – and we don't want to kill them off completely, do we? What's next?'

Charlie slid his eyes away from the garden and stared hard at my straight, brown hair.

I groaned.

'Oh, yeah, I forgot. Why does it have to be *thirteen* hairs?' I said. 'Why couldn't it be just one or two?'

I tugged at my head. By the time I had pulled out thirteen hairs, I was half-bald and nearly crying. But I mixed the hair into the rest of the potion, and chanted the rhyme out loud as I stirred.

Charlie miaowed sharply. I hid the jug behind a cactus plant just as Wormella returned to the kitchen.

For the rest of that morning, I slaved away in the steamy kitchen, chopping, cooking and cleaning. At one o'clock, a bell rang in the dining room.

'Where's our lunch?' shouted Grizz.

'It's coming!' I shouted back through gritted teeth. I balanced two plates of baked toad on my arm and glided into the dining room.

'About time. Tuck in, Wormella,' said Grizz.

Wormella viewed the steaming plate of toad in front of her with distaste. She wrinkled her nose.

'Oh dear,' she said. 'I seem to have lost my appetite.'

'I'm not surprised,' I said. Who was Wormella trying to kid? I'd seen her chomping on a cheeseburger earlier in the week when Grizz's back was turned.

'Silence, girl! Bring us some drinks,' said Grizz. She turned to her sister. 'How about some nettle wine, Wormella?'

Wormella cheered up instantly, and I hurried back into the kitchen.

'Now's my chance, Charlie!' I said. 'Charlie?'

That dopey moggy was lying on the worktop, snoring his furry head off. His paw was in the jug of sleeping potion, and there were traces of potion on his whiskers.

My mouth fell open. The potion had worked! I was really getting the hang of this witchy thing. Now all I had to do was get the potion into the aunts.

'Thanks, Charlie,' I said. 'But maybe you should keep your greedy snout out of it next time!'

I poured what was left of the potion into two wine glasses and topped them up with nettle wine. My hands were shaking all the while.

'Here we are, Aunts!' I said, as I placed the glasses in front of Grizz and Wormella. 'Two nettle wines!'

Grizz looked at me out of the corner of her eye. 'What are you so chirpy about?' she said. 'Get back to the kitchen and start clearing up. We'll ring when we need you.'

For five minutes, I paced up and down the kitchen as Charlie dozed. Then, I heard strange sounds coming from the dining room. I pressed my ear against the door.

'Fnagh, fnagh, fnagh,' snored one aunt.

'Hrumpphh, hrumpphh, hrumpphh,' snored the other.

I opened the door. Grizz was face down in the remains of her baked toad, and Wormella was lolling in her chair with drool dripping off her chin.

Yes! I shook my fist at them. Then I flung my stupid, pointy hat into a corner, and raced out of the dark house into the sunny street.

6

ST MUNCHIN'S

F ive minutes later, I was standing in front of
St Munchin's, I could hear my heart banging like a drum inside my tatty black dress. But it
was too late to turn back now. I slipped through
the iron gates, skirted around the playground and
peeped through some classroom windows.

After a while I spotted Mary. She was one of
about ten girls playing indoor football. She was
dribbling the ball; she was taking aim – she'd
scored! All her friends jumped on her as a frizzy-
haired teacher blew the whistle.

'Well done, girls!' she shouted.

I leaned my head against the window frame
and sniffed. Why wasn't I having fun with all
these other kids, instead of pulling my hair out in

a witch's kitchen? It wasn't fair.

'B r e a k--time!' called the teacher. 'Off you go!'

Most of the girls streamed out of the class – but Mary spotted me and waved. She came over to the classroom window and opened it.

'Hi, Anna!' she said. 'You managed to get away, then?'

'Yeah,' I said. 'It wasn't easy. I had to knock out my aunts.'

Mary put both hands over her mouth and

giggled. She still didn't believe me.

I peeped over her shoulder at the teacher.

'Won't she mind you talking to me?' I asked.

'Who, Miss Roland?' said Mary. 'No. She's cool – like most of the teachers here. The only one I'm a bit scared of is the head teacher, Mrs Winkle.'

Miss Roland came over to the window.

'Well, Mary,' she said. 'Who's your friend?'

'This is Anna, Miss,' said Mary. 'She lives on my road.' Mary shot me a sidelong glance. 'She wants to join St Munchin's.'

I chewed my lip and fiddled with the frayed sleeve of my black dress. I knew I wasn't making much of a first impression.

'Do you, Anna?' said Miss Roland to me.

'Yes, Miss,' I said.

'How very sensible,' said Miss Roland. 'But, somehow, I don't think you'll manage it by hanging around outside the window!'

She smiled, showing two deep dimples in her cheeks. I relaxed a little bit.

'Why don't you come in and have a look

around,' she said. 'Mary can show you her class-room.'

'Yes, Miss,' said Mary. She beckoned me through a side door.

As we walked down the corridor, I noticed that the walls were covered with pictures. There were bright notices flapping on boards.

'What are all those about?' I asked.

'They're activities,' said Mary. 'There's after-school swimming, choir, canoe lessons – there's even classes for adults.'

We slipped into a classroom that said 4B on the door.

'Ooooh!' I whispered, and I looked around. The place was covered with books, coloured paints, maps and toys – everything that was miss-ing from my life at Crag Road.

I could really picture myself here, sitting on top of one of the desks, laughing and talking with the other girls …

'Hello, girls!' boomed a voice behind us.

Mary and I both jumped out of our skin. We

turned around. A
large, white-
haired lady in a
blue suit was
standing in the
doorway.

Mary's eyes
opened wide.

'Mrs Winkle!'
she whispered.

Mrs Winkle peered at me over tiny glasses. Her
blue eyes seemed to bore into me, as if they could
see into my soul. I got fidgety.

'I think I'll be off now,' I said. 'Things to do.'

'Please don't go, Anna,' said Mrs Winkle. 'It's
not every day we get young people turning up
wanting to join our school!'

I looked at Mary.

'How did she know that?' I whispered. Mary
shrugged.

Mrs Winkle smiled. Her eyes glinted again.

'Not a lot goes on at St Munchin's that I don't

know about,' she said. She held the classroom door open. 'Will you come to my office, please? Mary, you can go.'

I gulped. I wasn't sure I was ready for this interview.

'Bye, Mary,' I mumbled, as I followed Mrs Winkle down the corridor.

'Good luck,' whispered Mary.

I trailed after Mrs Winkle down the long corridor.

'I'm sorry, Miss,' I said, as soon as I was inside Mrs Winkle's office. 'I didn't mean to barge in and disturb everyone.'

'I don't blame you for wanting to join our school, dear,' said Mrs Winkle, sitting down behind her desk. 'But, you know, this *is* an unusual way to go about it.'

'Trust me, Miss,' I said. 'I'm an unusual child.'

Mrs Winkle shook with silent laughter. She pulled a blue pen out of her bun and opened a register.

'Let's get some background,' she said. 'Where

do you live, Anna?'

'Number 13 Crag Road,' I said.

Mrs Winkle scribbled down this information.

'And with whom do you live?'

'I live with Grizz and Wormella Mint, my two adopted aunts.'

'Their occupation?' she said.

This was the part I'd been dreading.

'They're witches, Miss,' I said. 'Or at least they think they are.'

Mrs Winkle's head shot up and her eyes bored into me. Her smile had vanished and her face was deadly serious. I could suddenly see why Mary was a bit scared of her.

'I *beg* your pardon?' she said.

'My aunts think they're witches,' I said in a small voice.

'And do *you* think they're witches, Anna?' she said.

I shook my head.

'Not likely,' I said. 'Or, at least, if they are, they're the worst witches in the world.'

'How would *you* know?' said Mrs Winkle, her eyes glinting. 'Do you know much about witchcraft?'

'Well, no,' I admitted. 'But Grizz and Wormella

do have the pointy hats and the cauldron and all that …'

Mrs Winkle stroked her chin.

'Really?' she said. 'How very interesting.'

For some reason I couldn't seem to stop talking.

'And they *do* keep trying to do spells,' I gabbled. 'And none of them ever work. But *I* …'

I stopped and tried to get control of myself. After all, I didn't know if I could trust this big woman with the deep, blue eyes.

'Yes?' she said.

'Nothing,' I whispered and looked at the floor.

Mrs Winkle didn't question me further. She snapped the register shut and folded her hands.

'When can you start?'

My heart leapt. Was she letting me join? Was I really going to have friends, and play football, and win prizes …

'As soon as possible!' I said.

'I'll need to talk to your aunts, of course,' Mrs Winkle said.

My heart sank to my boots, but she smiled and

handed me a piece of paper.

'Take this home,' she said. 'And ask your aunts to sign it. I'll make a home visit as soon as I can.'

The last of my hopes trickled away. Grizz would never sign this – she would rather be boiled in her own cauldron than allow me to go to school.

'Please, Miss,' I said. 'Can't I … can't I sign it myself and save them the trouble?'

Mrs Winkle laughed again.

'Very good, Anna!' she said. 'That's what we like here at St Munchin's – a terrific sense of humour! We look forward to seeing you soon.' She picked up her pen and started to write.

I hung my head and turned away.

'Goodbye,' I whispered.

Trudging back to Crag Road, my thoughts circled round and round. I'd come *so* close to getting my wish. But it would all come to nothing. Grizz would see to that.

As I plodded closer to the house, I slowed down. What would be waiting for me? I hadn't

thought of that when I drugged Grizz and Wor-mella – and they would be awake by now…

I stood outside number 13, and gazed up at the sky. Clouds covered the sun and a cold wind was picking up. I had goosebumps all over my arms. I let myself in and crept into the kitchen.

Grizz and Wormella were sitting at the kitchen table – and Grizz was holding Charlie around the neck.

7

GRIZZ'S REVENGE

An hour later, Grizz was still shouting at me – and Wormella was still throwing up in the kitchen sink.

'I didn't do anything wrong!' I protested for the tenth time.

Grizz tightened her thin fingers around Charlie's neck. Charlie struggled and let out a strangled miaow.

'And I suppose poisoning your aunts and sneaking off isn't *wrong*?' said Grizz. 'Did your *walk* take you in the direction of St Munchin's, by any chance?'

'N-no,' I said. 'I went in the opposite direction.'

'*Liar!* How dare you tell me such a pack of lies!' screamed Grizz.

Charlie yowled in pain.

'*Please* let Charlie go!' I said. 'It's not *his* fault!'

'Where did you find that sleeping potion?' said Grizz.

'From that smelly old book you keep in the cellar,' I said. 'And I made the potion myself in your smelly old kitchen! It was *easy*!'

Wormella gasped.

'Her potion worked, sister!' she said. 'None of ours ever do! Do you think she could do ... other things?'

Grizz's eyes narrowed to grey slits. She pushed her face close to mine.

'Are you hiding something, girl?' she said. 'What else happened in the cellar?'

'Nothing,' I said. I was becoming an expert liar.

Grizz stared at me for a moment and then shook her head.

'No, no, Wormella,' she said. 'She may be able to cook a potion or two, but that's it. The gift of sorcery is not given to freckly little girls. It is given only to mature, clever women, like me, I mean, us.'

I itched to tell Grizz exactly what I knew – that I was a natural-born witch, and that I had only just begun to explore my powers. But it was safer to keep quiet.

'Listen to me, girl,' Grizz continued. 'You will never run away again. You will never touch my precious book again. You will stay here and work for me until you *die*, just like Wormella.'

'And if I don't?' I said.

'And if you don't,' said Grizz. 'It won't only be this mangy moggy that *suffers* ...'

I glanced at Wormella's bowed head under its frilly cap. Tears were splashing onto her plump hands.

'Anna, dear,' she whispered. 'Please do your training like a good girl. Otherwise ... otherwise Grizz gets cross with me, too.'

'Now get digging in the garden, both of you,' said Grizz.

'Yes, sister,' said Wormella.

My shoulders slumped. It was no good. I couldn't save Wormella, I couldn't save Charlie and I couldn't save myself. Grizz was too strong for me.

'Yes, Grizz,' I whispered.

What sort of witch was I, when I didn't even

know how to use my powers to defeat Grizz? I dragged myself through the kitchen door and out into the chilly garden.

Grizz kept me hard at work for the next three days – and kept poor little Charlie in a cage in the kitchen to make sure I did as I was told.

One evening, Mary knocked on the back door. Grizz shot me an evil look, and opened the door a tiny crack.

'Yes?' Grizz said.

'Can Anna come out to play?' Mary asked. Her voice was wobbly with nerves.

'No!' Grizz snapped. 'Clear off!'

And she slammed the door in Mary's face.

On the fourth day, I was cutting the guts out of a lizard and staring out of the kitchen window at the grey rain. There was a knock at the front door.

'That had better not be that little *friend* of yours again!' said Grizz.

Wormella trotted to the front of the house and peeked through a window.

'It's a big woman in a blue suit, dear,' she said.

I felt the sweat break out on the back of my neck, as Grizz's eyes bored into me.

Mrs Winkle was here! Maybe Mrs Winkle could *force* the aunts to send me to school! Maybe I could beg Mrs Winkle to take me away right now!

'Let her in, Wormella,' said Grizz, still staring at me.

While Wormella opened the front door, Grizz  darted over to me, grabbed me by the cheek and pulled me towards the back door.

'Ow!' I shouted. 'Where are you taking me *this* time?'

'No time to get you upstairs,' said Grizz. 'Out you go.'

Grizz dragged

me to the garden shed.

'No! Please, no!' I shouted. 'Don't lock me up again!'

Grizz pushed me though the door, and I toppled onto a heap of old broomsticks. By the time I had struggled to my feet, the key was already turning in the lock.

8

MRS WINKLE'S VISIT

'Let me out!' I shouted, bashing on the door. I heard Grizz's footsteps retreating up the garden, then the loud slam of the kitchen door.

I climbed onto the pile of broomsticks to look out of the shed's one and only window. It was a bit wobbly, but I could see the kitchen window and also hear what was going on.

Wormella bustled back into the kitchen.

'Mrs Winkle,' she announced.

Mrs Winkle strode into the middle of the room and gazed about her. Her eyes came to rest on the stove top, where the cauldron was bubbling.

'My, my,' she said. 'What a beautiful cauldron.'

'Yes, isn't it,' said Grizz. 'May I help you?'

Mrs Winkle ignored Grizz's question and stared hard at the purple steam billowing from the cauldron.

'Do you use it for anything … interesting?' she said.

Grizz frowned. I could tell it was a struggle for her to remain polite.

'Not really,' she said. 'Just the odd herbal remedy.'

'Such as?' said Mrs Winkle.

'Such as a treatment for baggy skin,' said Grizz. 'Can I offer you a cup – or perhaps a large mug might be more suitable in your case?'

'Mrs Winkle!' I shouted from the garden shed. 'Don't take anything from her!'

'What's that strange noise?' said Mrs Winkle. 'It sounded like banging or shouting.'

'It's mice,' said Grizz. 'Large ones. We're infested.'

'Really?' How unfortunate,' said Mrs Winkle. She looked out of the window and straight at me.

'Mrs Winkle!' I shouted. 'It's me! Let me out!'

I was sure that Mrs Winkle could see me jumping up and down. But if she did, she showed no sign. Instead she turned away to speak to Grizz again.

'I'll come straight to the point, Miss Mint,' she said. 'I believe Anna should be in St Munchin's.'

'But my sister and I are educating Anna at home,' said Grizz, smiling and linking arms with Wormella. 'Aren't we, sister?'

Wormella's mouth opened and closed like a goldfish, but no sound came out. Grizz pinched her hard on the elbow.

'Ouch! Yes, sister,' said Wormella.

Out in the shed, I leant my head against the window and closed my eyes.

'Wormella,' I groaned. 'When are you going to grow a backbone?'

'And what sort of *education* are you giving her?' said Mrs Winkle, running her eye over the jars and bottles on the shelves.

'The usual,' said Grizz. 'Maths, English, you know how it is.'

'Has she shown talent in any … *unusual* areas?' said Mrs Winkle.

'Such as?' said Grizz.

'Your herbal preparations, for example,' said Mrs Winkle. 'Does she enjoy helping you with those?'

'Dear me, no,' said Grizz. 'She's no help whatever. The child is far too stupid to pick up anything.'

'That remains to be seen,' said Mrs Winkle. 'In any case, we have one more place available this year. She has shown an interest and we'd love to have her.'

'Tch tch. What a waste of your valuable time,' said Grizz smoothly. 'You see, it's as I told you. Anna is far too headstrong to go to a big school. She needs ... special handling.'

Grizz and Mrs Winkle both crossed their arms and stared at each other across the kitchen table. Then Mrs Winkle sighed.

'There's nothing I can do without the permission of at least one of you,' she said. 'May I have a word with her?'

'She's out,' said Grizz. 'At her friend's house.'

Mrs Winkle sighed again.

'Miss Mint,' she said. 'If you change your mind, please make sure Anna comes by the end of the week. If she doesn't, I'm afraid I shall give her place to someone else.'

'Please *do*, Mrs Winkle,' said Grizz. 'Please *do* give Anna's place away to another little girl. She won't be needing it.'

'No!' I shouted, banging on the window frame. 'No, no, no!'

'There's that banging again,' said Mrs Winkle.

'Are you sure they're mice? They sound enormous ...'

Grizz took Mrs Winkle by the elbow and practically shoved her out of the kitchen.

'So nice of you to call,' she said. 'Goodbye.'

Seconds later, Grizz stormed down the garden path and into the shed. She grabbed me by the hair.

'Out, you minx!' she screeched. 'I'll teach you to bring disgrace to the house!'

'*Bring* disgrace!' I said. 'It wasn't exactly a model household to start with! Ow!'

Grizz dragged me into the house, up the stairs and into my attic, followed by a wittering Wormella.

'Don't hurt her, Grizz dear,' pleaded Wormella. 'She's so young ... don't hurt her.'

Grizz spun around to glare at Wormella and jabbed a finger in her face.

'Whose side are you on, Wormella?' she shouted.

Wormella shrank away from her sister.

I couldn't stand it anymore. Someone had to stand up for Wormella.

'Leave her alone!' I shouted at Grizz. 'You're nothing but a bully!'

'And as for *you*, girl,' said Grizz, turning back to me. 'We'll soon put a stop to this running-away-to-school nonsense,' She pushed me onto the bed and pointed her wand at the window.

'Bindweed root and cactus petal
Cover this glass with bars of metal.'

Nothing happened. There was an embarrassing silence.

'Rats!' shouted Grizz. 'Wormella, watch that girl!'

She stamped downstairs.

'Wormella,' I hissed. 'Stand up to Grizz! You *can* do it! You don't *have* to do everything she tells you.'

'Yes, I do, dear ...' whispered Wormella.

'If we banded together,' I said. 'We could have normal lives! We could eat normal food! We could

have friends …'

'No, no!' moaned Wormella, pressing her hands to her ears. 'Stop! I can't! It's all too late …'

It was no use. As soon as Grizz's footstep

sounded on the stair, Wormella scurried into a corner. Grizz entered, holding several planks of wood, a hammer and some nails. In five minutes, the wood was nailed over my window.

'It's bread and water for you tonight, my girl,' said Grizz. 'And no food for that fleabag feline friend of yours for a week!'

'You can lock us up and starve us all you want!' I shouted. 'I'm not going to work for you any more!'

'You will stay here until you go crazy,' said Grizz. 'Then we'll see whether you're willing to work or not. Come, Wormella.'

Grizz stamped out, followed by Wormella.

The tears started to fill my eyes as I crept to the boarded-up window. I blinked them away. Through a chink between the planks, I could just see Mary playing in her garden down the street.

9

WORMELLA'S SECRET

From my little attic room, I could hear Grizz calling Wormella bad names for a very long time. Occasionally there was the sound of breaking china. The worst bit was when I could hear Charlie crying in fear.

I could hardly bear to think what was going on. I paced up and down the attic. If only I could get out of this room.

I pointed at the door, and shouted the first rhyme that came into my head.

'Fart of dog and piglet's snout,
Open the door and let me out!'

Nothing happened. My powers were a bit

patchy, to say the least.

After dark, my door finally opened. Wormella shot into the room and plonked down a tray of bread and water.

'Oh dear, Anna,' she said. 'Oh dear, oh dear,' and burst into tears.

It was suspicious. I folded my arms and sat back on the bed.

'Did Grizz send you?' I asked.

'No, Anna, dear,' snivelled Wormella.

'Are you sure she doesn't want you to tug at my heartstrings?' I said. 'It's just the sort of sneaky thing she would do.'

Wormella sat on the edge of the bed.

'I-I-I just have to talk to someone,' she said. 'I don't know what to do anymore.'

Great. So now I was an agony aunt.

'Talk about what?' I said rudely. 'Trouble with one of your non-magic potions? Or have you suddenly noticed that we all live in a madhouse?'

'I-I-I don't know what to do about my sister,' said Wormella quietly.

I rolled my eyes. 'I think I've had quite enough of *her* for one day, thank you very much,' I said.

Wormella carried on as if I hadn't spoken.

'She's getting crosser and crosser every day,' she sniffed. 'And I know that it's never going to improve,' she said in a small voice. 'None of the spells are ever going to work because... because I know we're not witches really.'

My mouth fell open.

'You *know*?' I said. 'Since when?'

'Since ages ago,' gabbled Wormella. 'I never wanted to be a witch in the first place. I wanted to be an artist.'

'Why didn't you go to college to study?' I asked.

'I did. But then Grizz found *Ancient Evil* in a junk shop, and everything changed overnight,'

said Wormella. '*She* changed. She made me wear pointy hats and cook peculiar food and keep bats. She even made me change my name.'

Now I came to think of it, Wormella *was* rather a silly name. 'What's your real name?' I asked.

'It's Gladys,' said Wormella.

Laughter bubbled up inside me, but I pressed my lips tightly together to keep it in.

'What's Grizz's real name?' I asked.

'Betty,' said Wormella.

I bit back the laughter again.

Wormella was now unstoppable.

'I was going to study art in Paris and New York and everything,' she said.

'And you couldn't,' I said slowly. 'All because of Grizz and her book of evil spells.'

'Yes.' She started sniffling again. 'And now it's too late. I've wasted my life working for Grizz. I'm not strong enough to leave her, and anyway I'm too old to start again.'

I felt a wave of sympathy. I put my arm around

Wormella's shoulders.

'Cheer up, Aunty,' I said. 'It's *never* too late.'

I gazed through the chink in the planks towards the school. I sat up straight.

'Listen,' I said. 'I think I've got a plan.'

10

ANNA FIGHTS BACK

The next morning, I was already awake and dressed when the key sounded in the lock. A second later, Grizz stamped in.

'Time to get to work, girl,' she snapped. 'Don't give me any trouble. Chop chop.'

I leapt to my feet and stood to attention, smiling.

'Certainly, Aunt,' I said, and placed my pointy black hat on my head with care.

Grizz stared at me, confusion clouding her grey face. I beamed back at Grizz, then I skipped out of the attic and scampered down the stairs. Grizz followed, frowning.

'Morning, Aunty Wormy!' I chirped, as I skipped into the kitchen.

'Right, you two,' said Grizz. 'Enough of this chit-chat. Wormella, I want that spell cooked and bottled within the next ten minutes. And as for you, girl ...'

'Yes, Aunt?' I said, grinning at Grizz, who scowled back.

'I want you to wipe that smirk off your face, for a start,' she said. 'Make the beds and dust the furniture and wash the floors and, and ... oh, just get on with it.' Grizz threw a duster at me.

'Certainly, Aunt,' I said.

Once outside the kitchen door, I drew a deep breath. My plan was working so far. Grizz clearly couldn't stand the sight of me today, and now I had a few minutes to myself.

If I was going to act on my plan, it was now or never.

I tiptoed down the stairs, towards the cellar. I let myself in, lit a candle and glanced around.

Everything was just as it had been. Cobwebs hung in long strings from the ceilings and the animals' cages and tanks were again covered.

In the flickering candlelight, *Ancient Evil* looked more like a vicious animal than a book – one that was crouching on the worktop, ready to spring ...

I ran to the cages and tanks. I grabbed all the rags and threw them on the stone floor.

Inside the cages, the rats, mice and guinea pigs all squeaked in terror.

'Shh!' I said. 'I'm not here to hurt you!'

I fumbled with the cage doors and opened them one by one. Every creak from upstairs made my heart miss a beat. Finally, with trembling fingers, I flung open the last door on the last cage.

'Now's your chance!' I hissed. 'Run!' But the frightened little rodents just stared at me.

'Run, you dimwits!' I hissed.

I rattled all the cages. The animals scuttled in

every direction, diving into corners and searching for escape routes through the piles of rubbish.

I looked at the snakes curled up in the tanks. Their forked tongues slithered in and out of their mouths.

'Sorry, snakes,' I whispered. 'I'm not letting you go just yet. Maybe later – once I find out if you're poisonous!'

The maggot bucket was empty. I tried not to think about where *they* might be …

I picked up *Ancient Evil* and held it at arm's length. It weighed a ton and stank worse than a thousand rotten fish-heads. I dumped it in a metal bucket. It made a huge clatter, and my heart jumped into my throat.

Was that a sound on the stairs?

I had to work quickly – Grizz would come looking for me soon … I bent down and held the candle flame to the book's yellow pages.

'Let's see you magic your way out of this, you horrible thing,' I said.

I leapt back as *Ancient Evil* burst into flames

with a roar. Red, green and purple sparks flew up to the ceiling as it burned. There was a strange high-pitched squealing sound, as if some living thing was being burnt alive. As the pages blackened and curled, the sick flutter in my stomach died down.

Within seconds, the book had shrunk to a smouldering heap of ashes in the bucket. My eyes were watering from the smoke and stench, but I clenched my fists and turned back to the worktop.

'Now for the final job,' I muttered. I braced myself against a pillar, put both feet on the edge of the worktop and pushed with all my might.

'It gives me great pleasure …' I said through gritted teeth. 'To declare this laboratory …'

I strained as the whole thing tipped on one edge.

'BROKEN!' I shouted as the worktop crashed to the ground.

There was an ear-splitting sound of smashing glass as the bottles, dishes and jam jars all hit the stone floor and exploded in to a million pieces. The gooey green and yellow contents spilled everywhere, creating a lumpy, stinking, sizzling lake.

There was a heartbeat's silence. Then I heard the thud-thud-thud of footsteps racing towards the cellar.

11

MORE MAGIC

Grizz burst through the door, wild-eyed.
'My lab!' she cried. 'My own beautiful lab!'

She sank to her knees and gazed at the devastation. When she saw the remains of *Ancient Evil*, she screamed.

'My book!

My precious book!' she wailed.

Grizz buried her face in her hands. Sobs shook her thin shoulders. Wormella crept into the cellar. Her wide, shocked eyes met mine.

But I wasn't finished yet. I wanted Grizz to understand what it was like to feel small, and frightened, and alone.

I stepped inside one of the stars chalked on the ground. I pointed at Grizz and made up the first rhyme that came into my head,

'Snot of squid and leg of louse,
Turn Aunt Grizz into a mouse!'

After a heartbeat's silence, I felt a surge of power coming from the floor through my legs and into my whole body. There was a blinding flash of blue light.

When I opened my eyes, a thin, grey mouse was sitting on the step where Grizz had been.

Wormella screamed.

'Anna, what have you done?!' She pointed a shaking finger at me. 'You're a … you're a …'

'Witch,' I said. 'Yup, it certainly looks like it!'

I scooped up the mouse in my hand, and barged past Wormella. I ran up the steps and into the kitchen.

Charlie was sitting on the window sill. As soon as he saw the mouse, his back arched. His eyes narrowed to slits and he licked his lips. The mouse squealed and tried to run inside my sleeve.

Maybe I shouldn't have done it, but all I could think of was how cruel Grizz had been to me, and how lonely and unhappy I had been. I really, *really* wanted to get back at her.

So I dropped the mouse on the floor near Charlie. Then I walked out and slammed the door.

12

MRS WINKLE'S SECRET

It was playtime at St Munchin's. Across the play-ground, there were children screaming, laugh-ing, kicking foot-balls, and chasing each other. One small figure peeled off from the rest, and pelted across the

playground in my direction.

It was Mary.

'You're out!' she panted. 'I called at your house!'

'Yeah, I heard,' I said. 'So you met my aunt Grizz?'

'Yeah,' said Mary. She rolled her eyes. 'What a nightmare!'

'Tell me about it,' I said.

'So what's your next move?' said Mary.

'I've got to see Mrs Winkle again,' I said. 'I need her help and I've gone to a lot of trouble to get here today.'

'Here she comes now!' said Mary. She squinted at the large figure striding across the playground.

'She doesn't look too happy,' she said. 'I'm off!'

Mary raced across the playground and disappeared behind a tree. I straightened my shoulders, and turned to face Mrs Winkle.

'Anna Kelly!' she boomed.

'Good morning, Mrs Winkle,' I said. 'I have come to ask you ...'

Mrs Winkle peered over her glasses at me. Her blue eyes bored into my skull. She held up her hand and started counting on her fat fingers.

'First, you aren't in *school* when you should be,' she said. 'Then you aren't at *home* when you should be. Now you *are* in school when you shouldn't be ...'

'I'm sorry, Miss,' I said, slightly louder. 'But I've been a bit busy, what with learning magic, and getting locked up, and freeing animals, and destroying an evil book, and setting fire to cellars and ...'

Mrs Winkle held her hand up and I stopped talking. Her eyes glinted.

'Learning *what*?' she said. 'Did you say *magic*?'

I gulped. What had I said that for? She'd think I had really lost it and she'd have me locked up ...

But Mrs Winkle threw back her head and laughed.

'I knew it!' she said. 'I *knew* there was something *different* about you!'

There was something different about me all right – but how did Mrs Winkle know? As if

reading my mind, she leaned forward.

'Sometimes,' she whispered. 'It takes one to know one.'

My mouth fell open.

'You don't mean you're a …'

I couldn't quite get the word out, but Mrs Winkle nodded slowly.

'But you wear a suit,' I said. 'And you've got a proper job. You're a head teacher, for goodness sake!'

'Despite what your aunt Grizz thinks,' said Mrs Winkle, 'it's not all pointy hats and broom-sticks, not these days.'

She smiled.

'Come into my office. We have a lot to discuss …'

13

ANNA GOES HOME

T en minutes later, I was racing down the school corridor, past Miss Roland's class-room and out though the school gates.

I had just had the most interesting conversation of my life. Mrs Winkle told me all about modern witches, and how they didn't fly about on broom-sticks or eat frogs and toads, or even make spells in a cauldron!

She told me that she was a natural-born witch, like me. And she promised that if I went to school and worked hard, she would help me with my magic!

'Yippee!!' I shouted, as I raced down the road.

But back at 13 Crag Road, I leaned against the front door. I was worried. There was always a

result to any action – and now I had to face the results of my actions in the cellar.

'Oh, lordy,' I whispered. 'I only wanted to teach Grizz a lesson! I hope she's not dead!'

I heard a soft miaow and a rustle in the bushes and, a moment later, Charlie leapt out. He trotted over to me, purring like an engine. Was it my imagination or did he look a little fatter, as if he'd had a big meal?

'Oh Charlie,' I said. 'Please, *please* tell me you didn't *eat* Grizz.'

But Charlie just looked at me with innocent golden eyes and yawned. He was giving nothing away.

A lump formed in my throat. If Grizz was dead, it would be all my fault! I walked into the house and peeped around the kitchen door.

Wormella was sitting at the table as usual – but she was stroking something in her hand.

It was a thin, grey mouse.

'Thank goodness!' I said. A massive wave of relief washed over me. After all, I may be a witch, but I don't want to be a *murderer*!

'So *there* you are!' said Wormella. 'Anna, how *could* you?'

'Yes, Aunty?' I said.

'After you left,' said Wormella. 'I heard all this yowling and squeaking. So I rushed into the kitchen – and Charlie was throwing poor Grizz in the air over and over again!'

'Oops,' I said, trying to hide a smile.

'You *are* naughty, Anna,' scolded Wormella. 'She *is* my sister, after all.'

'She doesn't look like anybody's sister at the moment,' I said. 'And it serves her right. She's been really horrible to me, you know.'

'I know,' said Wormella. 'But she's not really that bad underneath. It was *Ancient Evil* that did it.'

Wormella put her hands over the mouse's ears.

'And I'm glad it's gone!' she whispered.

'My pleasure, Aunty,' I said, bowing.

'But Anna,' said Wormella. 'You should have *told* me you were a witch.'

'I didn't know myself until a few days ago,' I said.

'Well,' said Wormella firmly, 'You can just use your powers to turn this rodent back into my sister.'

'I'll do my best, Aunty,' I said. 'But I'm just sort of making it up as I go along.'

I took some white chalk from the kitchen drawer and drew a five-pointed star on the floor. Then I stepped inside, and pointed my right index finger at the grey mouse, I tried hard to think of rhyme that would change it back into Grizz.

Nothing came to me. My mind was completely blank. I stood there for ages until my legs went numb.

'Well?' said Wormella.

'I'm really sorry, Aunty,' I said. 'Nothing seems to be happening.' I stepped out of the star and sat down. 'I don't think I'm very good yet.'

'You can say that again,' said Wormella. She sighed and stroked the little grey mouse. 'Grizz really is quite sweet like this, though, isn't she?'

'A lot nicer, in my opinion,' I said.

Our eyes met.

'No, Anna,' said Wormella. 'We can't just *leave* her like this!'

'But she'll be all right for a while,' I said. 'At least until I can work out how to change her back. And it would certainly give her plenty of time to think about her evil ways.'

'I suppose so,' said Wormella. 'Just make sure you keep Charlie away from her.'

I took the mouse from Wormella and wagged my finger at it.

'You can stay in one of the old cages, Grizz,' I said. 'And after I turn you back – *if* I turn you back – you'd better behave!'

The mouse squeaked a bit and stuck its nose in the air. I handed it back to Wormella.

'What now, Anna?' said Wormella. She lowered her eyes and her chins began to wobble. 'I expect you'll want to leave, won't you?'

'No, Aunty,' I said. 'I'm staying.'

'Really?' said Wormella, beaming.

'But there are going to be a lot of changes around here,' I said. 'I'm going to St Munchin's, and I'm going to make friends and have a normal life – that is, as normal as possible in the circumstances. You're not going to try and stop me, are you?'

Wormella looked at me to the mouse and back to me.

'Wouldn't dream of it, dear,' she said. 'In fact, I feel quite jealous. I'd love to go back to school.'

I had a bright idea.

'Why *don't* you, then!' I said. 'There are loads of evening classes for adults at St Munchin's!'

Wormella's mouth dropped open.

'Could I, Anna?' she whispered. 'Could I, really?'

'Yes!' I said. 'You could sign up for an art class, like you always wanted! And let's face it,' I poked the mouse with my finger, '*she's* not going to be able to do anything about it, is she?'

'I suppose not,' Wormella said, giggling.

'And even when I manage to change Grizz back into human form,' I said, 'She still won't be able to do anything to us.'

'Why's that, dear?'

'Let's just say I've got to know some powerful people…' I said.

Wormella's eyes went wide and curious.

'Who on earth do you mean?' she said.

I tapped the side of my nose, which meant

'mind your own business'. I didn't want to get in trouble with Mrs Winkle for blabbing about her.

'Sorry, Aunty,' I said. 'Can't tell you at the moment. Top-secret.'

'Very well, dear,' said Wormella. 'If you say so.'

She put the mouse on the table, got up and put her apron on.

'Well, I can't sit about chatting all day,' she said. 'Your tea isn't going to make itself, you know. Sausage and chips all right, dear?'

Sausage and chips! At last! A decent meal! It sounded like music to my ears.

'Yes, please!' I said. 'But, first, I've just got to pop outside for a second.'

I ran into the garden to the dustbin. I lifted the dustbin lid, took off my black hat, and threw it in. Then, with a smile, I slammed the lid shut and ran back inside.